Sammy Goes to the Doctor

Written by
Brittany Feria

Illustrated by
Wandson Rocha

Blue Balloon Books
An Imprint of Ballast Books, LLC
www.blueballoonbooks.com
www.ballastbooks.com

Copyright © 2025 by Brittany Feria
Illustrations by Wandson Rocha, represented by Beehive Illustration

All rights reserved. No part of this book may be reproduced in any form or by any electronic or mechanical means, including information storage and retrieval systems, without permissionin writing from the publisher, except by reviewers, who may quote brief passages in a review.

ISBN: 978-1-966786-10-8

Printed in Hong Kong

Published by Blue Balloon Books
www.blueballoonbooks.com

To my children, who provide me with endless stories.

Sammy's mommy comes into his room and gives him a big kiss. "Time to wake up, Sammy. We have to go to the doctor today."

"Uh, no, we don't. I went there yesterday, remember?" asks Sammy.

"Silly Sammy, no, you didn't. Brush your teeth! It's time to go," says Mommy.

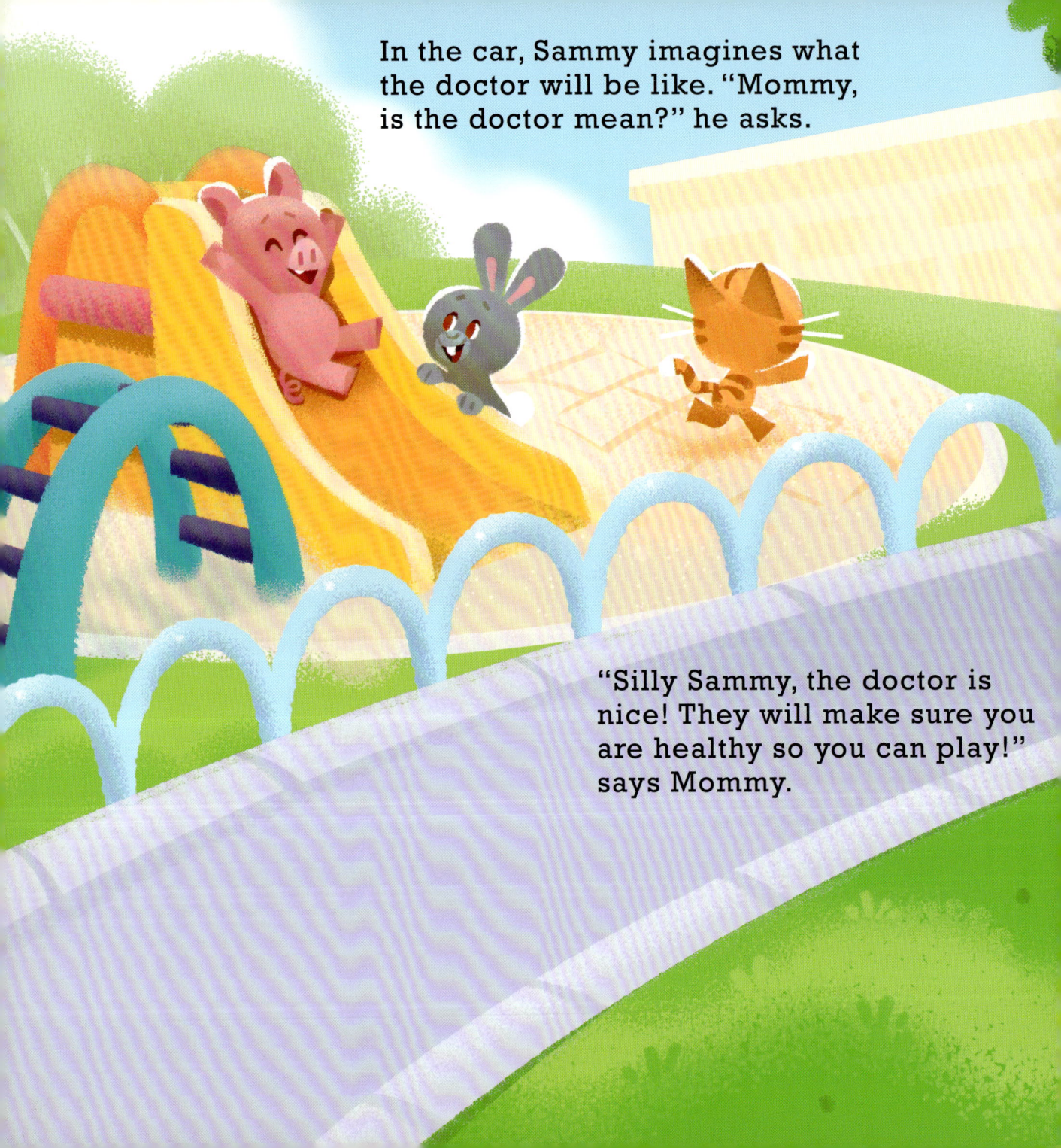

In the car, Sammy imagines what the doctor will be like. "Mommy, is the doctor mean?" he asks.

"Silly Sammy, the doctor is nice! They will make sure you are healthy so you can play!" says Mommy.

Well, I do like to play, Sammy thinks.

At the doctor's office, there are a lot of toys to play with.

"Hey, this place looks fun! Bye, Mom!" Sammy yells as he runs to the toys.

After playing, Sammy returns to his mom. "Okay, Mommy, the doctor was fun. We can go home now."

"Silly Sammy, we haven't seen the doctor yet! We have to wait until they call your name," Mommy explains.

Just then, a nurse opens the door and calls, "Sammy?"

Mommy takes Sammy's paw, and they follow the nurse into a different room.

"Okay, Sammy, let's see how much you've grown!" the nurse says, pointing to a scale.

Sammy grabs his mommy's leg. "I'm scared, Mommy."

"It's okay, my Silly Sammy. I'm right here, and I won't let anything bad happen to you. This nurse is going to measure how tall you are and see how much you weigh," Mommy explains.

Sammy slowly steps on the scale.

"WOAH! You've gotten so big! Good job, Sammy!" exclaims the nurse.

Sammy smiles. He has gotten big!

Next, the nurse asks Sammy's mommy what he eats, how much he exercises, and how much juice he drinks. What silly questions!

Finally, the nurse leaves the room.

"**Wahoo!** We can go home now!" Sammy cheers.

"Silly Sammy, we still haven't seen the doctor!" Mommy says.

Gee, there sure are a lot of steps when you go to the doctor, Sammy thinks.

KNOCK, KNOCK!

The door swings open, and in walks a stranger in a white coat.

"Hello, Sammy. I'm your doctor! I'm going to listen to your heart," the stranger says.

The doctor shows Sammy his stethoscope.

"I am going to use this to listen to your heart. Is that OK?"

Sammy nods.

The doctor presses the stethoscope to Sammy's chest. It's a little cold, but it doesn't hurt at all!

"Good job, Sammy. You sound really healthy! The nurse will be back soon with your vaccines."

"YAY! Let's go home," yells Sammy.

"Silly Sammy, we have to wait for your shots!" Mommy explains.

Sammy isn't sure what shots are, but he's sure he doesn't like them.

After a few minutes, the nurse comes back in. "Okay, Sammy," she says, "you're going to feel a little pinch, but since you are a big, strong kid, you're going to be brave for me, right?"

"OUCH!" Sammy shouts.

Mommy laughs. "Silly Sammy, the nurse didn't give you the shot yet! She was just cleaning your arm."

"Oh, I guess I was just scared," Sammy explains, laughing too.

While Sammy talks to his mommy, the nurse gives him his shot. He doesn't even notice!

"All done!" the nurse says.

Wow, that wasn't so bad! Sammy thinks. *Shots aren't scary after all.*

Then, the nurse gives Sammy a bandage for his arm. It's Sammy's favorite color—blue!

"Okay, who do we have to wait for now?" Sammy asks.

"Silly Sammy, we get to go home! We're all done!" Mommy answers.

"YAAAAAAAAY!" cheers Sammy.

On their way out of the office, the receptionist gives Sammy a sticker and a balloon! Balloons are his favorite.

"Going to the doctor is actually fun," Sammy tells his mom. He shows her his bandage, sticker, and balloon. They're awesome!

Back at home, Sammy loves playing doctor.

"Time for your shot, Mommy!" says Sammy.

"Silly Sammy, I love you," says Mommy, smiling.

"Mommy," Sammy says, "I'm not Sammy! I'm the doctor. Now, it's time for your shot!"

THE END